Acting Ed

MW01198857

Lost Girl

by Kimberly Belflower

ǁ SAMUEL FRENCH ǁ

FOR PRODUCTION INQUIRIES
UNITED STATES AND CANADA
info@concordtheatricals.com
1-866-979-0447

UNITED KINGDOM AND EUROPE
licensing@concordtheatricals.co.uk
020-7054-7298

Each title is subject to availability from Concord Theatricals Corp., depending upon country of performance. Please be aware that *LOST GIRL* may not be licensed by Concord Theatricals Corp. in your territory. Professional and amateur producers should contact the nearest Concord Theatricals Corp. office or licensing partner to verify availability.

LOST GIRL was originally performed as a workshop production through Texas Performing Arts at the University of Texas at Austin in November 2016. The performance was directed by Cara Phipps, with assistant direction by Kevin Poole, set design by Camryn de Wet, costume design by Kelsey Vidic, lighting design by Yi-Tai Chung, projection design by Jon Haas, sound design by Joseph Cornelison, and movement direction by Kelsey Oliver. The dramaturg was Cortney McEniry, the community engagement coordinator was Lauren Smith, the production stage manager was Jessica Forte, and the assistant stage manager was Josh Secor. The cast was as follows:

WENDY	Adriana Scamardi
CORA / A	Toni Lorene Baker
MOTHER / B	Kat Lozano
CALLIE / C	Jordan Maranto
NINA / D	Annemarie Alaniz
SLIGHTLY / DETECTIVE	Josh Cole
CURLY / THERAPIST	Steven Schwope
NIBS / DOCTOR	Ismael Vallejo
TOODLES / BOY	Teddy Santiesteban
PETER	Luke Stodghill

LOST GIRL had its world premiere at Milwaukee Repertory Theater (Mark Clements, Artistic Director; Chad Bauman, Managing Director) through the Professional Training Institute and the John (Jack) D. Lewis New Play Development Program in July 2018. The performance was directed by Ryan Quinn and produced by Cortney McEniry and Nabra Nelson, with costume design by Alexander B. Tecoma, lighting design by Marisa Abbot, sound design by Erin Paige, and properties direction by James Guy. The dramaturg was Deanie Vallone, the music director was Patrick Budde, the stage movement director was Desiree Cocroft, the casting director was Frank Honts, the production stage manager was Kyle Winkelman, and the assistant stage manager was Kai Liebenstein. The cast was as follows:

WENDY . . . . Reese Parish

CORA / A . . . . Mainyia Xiong

CALLIE / B . . . . .Maricella Kessenich

KRISTA / C . . . . .Juliana Garcia-Malacara

NINA . . . . .Meguire Hennes

MOTHER . . . . Saleaqua Winston

SLIGHTLY . . . . Kenyon Terrell

NIBS / DETECTIVE . . . . Logan Muñoz

CURLY / DOCTOR . . . . Dominic Schiro

TOODLES / THERAPIST . . . . Durran Goodwin, Jr.

BOY . . . . Bradley Nowacek

PETER . . . . Elliott Brotherhood

CHARACTERS

WENDY – Female, 18–20, sometimes 13–14ish. A storyteller. She might gravitate toward melancholy, but she's still openhearted and hopeful, with an undercurrent of tough determination.

PETER – Male, 13ish, then 18–20. Always well-intentioned and so charismatic you could just die. He's not a villain. He's just a boy.

A / B / C – Female, 16–22. Chorus. Different versions of Wendy from her past, memories distorted through time, and other girls who went to Neverland. All of the above.

MOTHER – Female, 40s. Tired, thoughtful, and patient.

CORA – Female, 16–22. No-nonsense.

CALLIE – Female, 16–22. Romantic but self-aware.

KRISTA – Female, 16–22. Empathetic.

NINA – Female, 16–22. Curious and kind.

SLIGHTLY – Male, 18–22. Careful, caring, and fiercely loyal.

TOODLES – Male, 16–22. Silly and sincere.

NIBS – Male, 18–22. Logical. Acerbic.

CURLY – Male, 16–22. Laid-back but observant.

DETECTIVE – Male, 30s–40s. Single-minded, always on the edge of defeat.

THERAPIST – Male, 30s–40s. Trying his best.

DOCTOR – Male, 30s–40s. Even-tempered.

BOY – Male, 18–25. Quiet confidence.

The following roles should be doubled:

CORA / A
CALLIE / B
KRISTA / C
CURLY / DOCTOR
NIBS / DETECTIVE
TOODLES / THERAPIST

SETTING

Wendy's room, the nursery. There is a large window that always remains, no matter where else we go.

Offices of the Detective, Doctor, and Therapist.

The Boy's bed.

Yards with laundry lines.

Neutral places like coffee shops and park benches.

Neverland.

The set should allow for fast, fluid transitions.

AUTHOR'S NOTES

A Note on Doubling

Wendy's memory and reality are deeply intertwined. While the play can be done with eighteen actors instead of twelve, the noted doubling is preferable for storytelling purposes.

A Note on Casting

It is absolutely essential for this play to be cast with a diversity of actors. Professional and amateur non-school productions should cast at least fifty percent actors of color. Amateur school productions should come as close to this percentage as possible.

Gender presentation is noted, but casting non-binary and trans people in these roles is encouraged. Lost Boys, especially, need not be played by cisgender men.

A Note on Time

J.M. Barrie's *Peter Pan* was written and set in 1900s England. This play is not. It should feel contemporary but also a little bit out of time entirely, in the way that living in your head tends to feel. Time doesn't move in a straight line.

Punctuation and Pacing

A slash (/) indicates an overlap in speech. Whenever a (/) appears, the next line of dialogue should immediately begin. A dash (–) notes a thought being interrupted, whether by another thought or by another character. Ellipses (…) note a thought trailing off, or a thought that's not yet fully formed.

The play should move quickly and run no longer than an hour and twenty minutes. Transitions between scenes happen within the world of the play and work best when actor-activated.

Use line breaks, capitalization, and punctuation as clues for breath, importance, and pace.

This play is dedicated to the memory of Gail Jones.
Thank you for finding me.

With special thanks to:
SJD, for giving me – and this play – motion.
Liz, for listening and leading (I will follow).
Cortney, for always believing and understanding.
Cara, for Posse (which means a lot of things).
Kevin, for the earth to my water.
Alison and Blake, for growing up with me.
Jeff and Katie and Henry and Mom and Dad, for everything.

"When I loved him it felt like light
Coming out of my skin. I don't mean this
In a good way."

– Meg Freitag, "A Relationship in Chiarascuro"

" 'Which did you like best of all?'
'I think I liked the home under the ground best of all.'
'Yes, so do I. What was the last thing Peter ever said to you?'

'The last thing he ever said to me was,

Just always be waiting for me...' "

– J.M. Barrie, *Peter Pan*

(A spare stage.)

(A large window.)

WENDY. The first time I saw him, I saw his shadow first.
I was pretending to be asleep
but I wasn't asleep.
It was around the time I stopped thinking that staying
up late was a victory.
It was an awfully long time ago.

(Years ago.)

A. Did you hear –?

B. Did you know –?

C. About the girl –

BOY. Wendy –

NINA. That girl and her two brothers –

A. Michael –

C. John –

THERAPIST. All three children –

B. Gone.

A. Taken.

DETECTIVE. We don't know if they were taken.

THERAPIST. They're only children, they couldn't have gone
far on their own.

BOY. The window was open.

DOCTOR. But the doors were still locked.

B. Can you imagine?

C. I just can't even imagine.

A. Their poor mother.

*(The **DETECTIVE** and Wendy's **MOTHER**.)*

(Eight days after the children disappeared.)

(The **DETECTIVE** *reviews paperwork.)*

DETECTIVE. They've been gone for –
> How long?
> One week?

MOTHER. Eight days.

> *(The* **DETECTIVE** *makes a note.)*

DETECTIVE. We're optimistic that some of our leads will pay off soon.
> Now please, just one more time.
> Was there anything different about that night?
> The last time you saw them?

MOTHER. It was supposed to be Wendy's last night in the nursery.
> They were in their beds.
> Side by side by side.
> "The Nursery" is a leftover name from a long time ago.
> They've all slept in the same room since they were babies.
> But it was time.
> Wendy was at That Age.

DETECTIVE. What age is that?

MOTHER. When everything changes.
> When everything matters.
> Anything that happens –
> It's bigger than it would have been before.
> Than it will be after.
> It gets into your bones and it doesn't leave.
> It starts around the time you stop wearing bows in your hair.

> *(***WENDY** *and* **PETER** *in Neverland.)*
> *(They're both thirteen-ish.)*
> *(Every feeling is new.)*

WENDY. Why is it called Neverland?
> Why not Foreverland?

PETER. We can change the name if you want to.

WENDY. I suppose they're different versions of the same thing.

Never.

Forever.

They're both promises.

PETER. Oh, Wendy Darling.

WENDY. Yes, Peter Pan?

PETER. Nothing.

I like saying your name.

It feels as pretty to say as you are to look at.

WENDY. …I want to give you something.

PETER. What?

WENDY. What would you like?

PETER. Whatever you want to give me.

WENDY. But I want to give you something you like.

PETER. I'll like it.

WENDY. How do you know?

PETER. I know.

WENDY. How about a kiss?

PETER. What's that?

WENDY. Surely you know what a kiss is.

PETER. Oh, that's right.

Didn't you already give me one of those?

WENDY. This is a different kind of kiss.

I've never given one before.

PETER. I'll take good care of it.

WENDY. It's not that kind of gift, silly.

PETER. Oh.

You're going to want it back, aren't you?

People always give things, and then they always want them back.

WENDY. No.

I won't want this back.

I want you to keep it.
Here –

> (**WENDY** *moves toward* **PETER.**)
>
> (*The moment dissolves.*)
>
> (**PETER** *disappears.*)

I give myself eight minutes a day to think about him.
To remember.
Uninterrupted. Without feeling guilty or mad at myself.
It seems a reasonable amount of time –
Eight is my favorite number.
I've whittled it down over the years.
Maybe one day it'll be five minutes.
Then two.
Then no minutes at all.

A. Did you hear –?

B. Do you know –?

C. That girl.

BOY. What was her name again?

THERAPIST. Those children.

B. The ones who were gone.

DETECTIVE. They're back.

NINA. Where did they go?

DOCTOR. What was the word?

BOY. It sounded made-up.

A, B & C. Neverland.

WENDY. He said come away with me.
    He said forever.
    I said
    That's an awfully long time
    and I guess we were just saying pretty words
    Even though it felt Big and Real.
    We were kids, you know.
    Kids say things.

He was a boy.

I was a girl.

Boys make big promises.

Girls know better than to believe them,

but they go along with them anyway.

…

I went along with him anyway.

DETECTIVE. No official statement has been given.

THERAPIST. But the girl –

A. Something's wrong with her, they say.

B. They say she won't speak.

C. They say she can't speak.

A. Her eyes are wild, they say.

NINA. She can't stop crying, they say.

WENDY. The first time I kissed him, it felt more like flying than flying did.

The last time I kissed him was the last time I saw him.

I didn't know it was the last time.

It was just another kiss.

A. She doesn't sleep, they say.

B. She sleeps all day.

A. She wakes at night.

C. Her hair was filthy –

B. Twigs and leaves and mud.

NINA. What a nightmare.

WENDY. He said he'd be back.

He said I should wait.

And I did.

I do.

Because he said I should.

B. She brought all these boys with her –

(*The* **LOST BOYS** *gather around* **WENDY**.)

C. Strange boys –

B. With strange names –

A. They sounded made-up.

NINA. Just like that place.

C. Toodles?

A. Nibs?

B. Curly?

C. Slightly?

A. What kinds of names are those?

B. None of them wore any shoes –

C. Their hair grown into clumps –

A. They had all been taken, too, she claimed.

B. Children, taken away from their warm beds.

C. Away from their mothers and fathers who loved them.

B. Away through the window, just like that.

A. Where did they come from?

C. How did they get there?

A. Why did she bring them back?

B. What are they going to do now?

NINA. What is *she* going to do now?

WENDY. When he flew away that last time, it started to
    snow.

    It was never winter there – where he lived –

    It was part of the magic, somehow.

    He told me once, he said,

    "It's only winter when I go away."

    And he was right.

        (Snow.)

        *(**MOTHER** comes in.)*

        *(She watches **WENDY** for a moment.)*

MOTHER. Are you all right?

WENDY. Yes, Mother.

MOTHER. I thought I heard crying in the hall.

WENDY. It must have been the maid.

MOTHER. We don't have a maid.

WENDY. We used to.

MOTHER. Your voice sounds discouraged.

Are you discouraged?

WENDY. I'm tired.

MOTHER. You slept all day.

WENDY. No, I didn't.

I just stayed in my room.

MOTHER. I thought you were sleeping.

WENDY. I was being sad.

MOTHER. It's fine to be sad…

WENDY. Thank you.

That's not what I thought you'd say.

MOTHER. But Wendy, dear, you're Always sad.

It's not fine to be Always sad.

WENDY. I'm not always sad.

MOTHER. I was understanding at first, but it's gotten out of hand.

It's become a problem, and it's time to do something about it.

WENDY. I am doing all kinds of things about it.

I just haven't found anything that works.

MOTHER. I've decided to turn the nursery into an office.

(Beat.)

I've wanted one for years.

If you want to stay here, you can move to one of the downstairs rooms.

Some change will do you good.

(Pause.)

WENDY. No.

MOTHER. It's not a question.

WENDY. It's my *room*.

MOTHER. It has become more than a room.

It's a fixation.

You still keep the window open, after all these years.
You –
Your doctors and I all agree.
It's time.

WENDY. Why have you been talking to my doctors?!
This is crazy!
I *like* the window open, it has nothing to do with –

MOTHER. I am doing the best I know how to help you be happy.

WENDY. Why does everyone have to be happy?
When did that become the goal?
Maybe I don't like being happy.
I don't trust it.
Because as soon as you feel happiness, it's already gone
And who knows if you can ever get it back.
There's this Pressure
To remember every detail –
Everything that led up to that exact happiness –
So I can follow the steps and make it happen all over again.
And then I do that –
I follow the steps.
And it's never quite the same.
Even when it's good
It's not *as* good.
Or if it's *as* good
It's a different *kind* of good.
I always end up disappointed.
And after a while
I guess I got used to that disappointment.
It's nice to be used to something.

So I'm sorry you think being sad is a problem.
But for me, happiness is the problem.
It aches and it breaks and it leaves.

Sadness, though.

Sadness stays.

It's sturdy, and it's strong.

It burrows into your shoulder –

It stays all night.

> *(Beat.)*
>
> *(Then* **MOTHER** *leaves for a moment.)*
>
> *(She comes back with an armful of cardboard boxes –)*
>
> *(Some assembled, some flat.)*
>
> *(She sets them down.)*
>
> *(She leaves.)*
>
> *(Beat.)*

I give myself eight minutes a day to think about him. To remember.

> *(She remembers.)*

They asked me a lot of questions when I got back.

> *(Years ago.)*
>
> *(The detective's office.)*
>
> *(Wendy returned from Neverland two days earlier.)*

DETECTIVE. Were they in danger? These boys?

Is that why you brought them with you?

WENDY. No.

DETECTIVE. Was it him?

Peter?

> *(***WENDY*** says nothing.)*

Where does he live?

WENDY. You won't find him.

DETECTIVE. What if you showed us the way?

WENDY. Can you fly?

DETECTIVE. Can you?

WENDY. I could.

I don't think I can anymore.

DETECTIVE. That sounds dangerous.

WENDY. It is.

Was.

DETECTIVE. What can you tell me about him?

(**WENDY** *looks away.*)

(*Says nothing.*)

A. He loves stories.

B. One night I heard him crying when he thought I was asleep.

C. I never asked why.

DETECTIVE. Wendy? Did you hear me?

What can you tell me about him?

WENDY. Nothing.

DETECTIVE. Did he hurt you?

WENDY. What do you mean?

DETECTIVE. Answer the question.

WENDY. There are a lot of ways to be hurt.

I think you're asking about a specific way.

Aren't you?

DETECTIVE. Three young children disappear…

We can't help but make assumptions.

WENDY. Making assumptions is symptomatic of a faulty imagination.

DETECTIVE. Mighty big words.

Your mother said how smart you are.

WENDY. No.

He didn't hurt me like that.

I fell down and scraped my knee and my elbow, though.

When we were running one night.

See?

DETECTIVE. What were you running from?

WENDY. We were running *to*, not from.

DETECTIVE. What were you running to?

C. A fairy dance.

B. A pirate ship.

A. A mermaid lagoon.

B. There wasn't a mermaid lagoon.

C. Was there?

A. Of course there was – how could you forget?

WENDY. Who can remember.

There was always so much.

We were always running.

DETECTIVE. Tell me more.

WENDY. It was magical.

And scary.

DETECTIVE. Scary how?

WENDY. Why don't you ask about how it was magical?

Everyone wants to know about scary, no one wants to
know about magical.

DETECTIVE. Okay, then, how was it magical?

WENDY. Literally.

There was magic everywhere.

In the air, in the water, in the trees...

We had to keep a careful eye on the trees –

Their shadows sneak up on you if you aren't careful.

Shadows are different there –

There's an entire colony of them.

Peter's gets away from him all the time and he –

(The **DETECTIVE** *makes a note.)*

I know you don't believe me.

DETECTIVE. I didn't say that.

(Beat.)

And how was it scary?

WENDY. Because of the magic.

Because it was everywhere.

Because of him.

C. I had never felt those kinds of feelings.

A. They were so big, it felt dangerous.

B. There are two groups of people in this world –

A. Those who shine with a holy light,

C. And those who notice.

A. He shone.

B. I noticed.

DETECTIVE. Your mother says that you've been different since you came back

And that John and Michael are the same as before.

Do you think that's true?

WENDY. You ask a lot of questions.

DETECTIVE. That's my job.

WENDY. Pretty easy job.

Can I try?

DETECTIVE. Ask away.

WENDY. How long was I gone?

DETECTIVE. How long do you think you were gone?

WENDY. A year?

(Beat.)

Longer?

DETECTIVE. Nine days.

(Beat.)

WENDY. Oh.

(A long pause.)

*(**WENDY** digests this information.)*

DETECTIVE. Your mother said you haven't stopped crying. Why?

WENDY. People cry.

Life is hard.

Don't bother looking.

You won't find him.

He does the finding.

(A doctor's office.)

*(The **DOCTOR** checks **WENDY**'s glands.)*

DOCTOR. Open.

*(**WENDY** opens her mouth.)*

*(The **DOCTOR** peers in.)*

Say "ahhhhh."

WENDY. Ahhhhhhhhhhhh.

*(The **DOCTOR** puts a tongue depressor inside **WENDY**'s mouth.)*

(Looks.)

B. The first time I saw him
I screamed.

A. He was at my window,

B. And I don't live on the ground floor.

C. To be perfectly honest, it was all a bit frightening.

*(The **DOCTOR** takes out the tongue depressor.)*

DOCTOR. Good.
Now close.

*(**WENDY** closes her mouth.)*

Good.

*(The **DOCTOR** checks **WENDY**'s eyes with an ophthalmoscope.)*

A. I don't believe anything a boy tells me.

C. Or
I believe everything a boy tells me.

B. It's never in between.

*(The **DOCTOR** presses on **WENDY**'s chest, her head.)*

(He prepares a stethoscope.)

DOCTOR. Deep breath
In.

*(**WENDY** takes a deep breath in.)*

C. It was around the time candy started hurting my stomach.

DOCTOR. Out.

>   (**WENDY** *lets a deep breath out.*)

Good.

WENDY. My shadow's too heavy.

>   Can you fix it?

DOCTOR. Shadows don't weigh anything.

WENDY. Mine does.

>   And it's getting bigger.

A. Shadows stick around.

B. They follow you.

C. All the things you hold on to.

A. All the lives you don't lead

C. But almost led.

B. Some people don't have shadows.

C. Why not?

A. They don't hold on to things.

B. They shed themselves like snakes.

WENDY. I don't Feel normal.

DOCTOR. Feelings are not part of my job.

>   (**WENDY** *and a* **THERAPIST.**)

THERAPIST. So you feel he took something tangible from you?

>   Something you could touch, something you could lose?

WENDY. I guess.

THERAPIST. How does that make you feel?

WENDY. Empty.

THERAPIST. And how do you think that makes him feel?

WENDY. Full.

>   (*Beat.*)

THERAPIST. I know this has all been quite overwhelming, Wendy.

Doctors and detectives. Newspapers and questions.
I don't want you to think of me as your therapist.
I want you to think of me as your friend.
Someone you can talk to.

> (**WENDY** *says nothing.*)

> (*The* **THERAPIST** *waits patiently then can't take it anymore.*)

Do you want to tell me anything else about him?

WENDY. No thank you.

THERAPIST. What about your parents?

WENDY. I don't have any.

THERAPIST. Yes, you do. Your mother is waiting in the lobby.

WENDY. What if I told you she wasn't my mother?

THERAPIST. Wendy.

WENDY. You're no fun.

> (*The* **THERAPIST** *makes a note.*)

> (*Beat.*)

Did she tell you my dad left?

THERAPIST. She did.

WENDY. Yeah.

> (*Beat.*)

THERAPIST. That must be very hard.
Especially on top of everything else.

WENDY. I haven't paid it much attention.
I have a hard time focusing on more than one feeling at the same time.

THERAPIST. I'm sure you've paid it some attention.
What have you noticed? What's different?

WENDY. Well.
John and Michael went with him.
They didn't like everyone talking about them.
Clean break. Fresh start.

They were louder than me,

so it's quieter now.

And he was big, my father.

So the house has kind of – opened up.

THERAPIST. Big how?

WENDY. In every way.

Tall.

Fat.

Big laugher.

Big talker.

Big thinker.

But he could fill you up with his bigness,

or he could use it to make you feel small.

So now there's this big emptiness he left behind

and everything else is a different size...

I guess my mom and I always hid behind him, on different sides?

And we never really had to look at each other until he was gone.

So it's good that all this other stuff is going on.

It's good that she has to bring me here, to talk to you.

Now we have other things to hide behind.

(Time passes.)

A. Did you hear –?

BOY. Do you remember –?

B. That girl.

DETECTIVE. Wendy Darling.

C. How old is she now?

A. Old enough.

B. She grew up.

C. She's *growing* up.

DOCTOR. They say she hardly leaves the house.

C. Still.

THERAPIST. They say she cries all the time.

B. Still.

DETECTIVE. They say she doesn't sleep.

A. Still.

NINA. They say she doesn't have any friends.

C. Besides those boys.

B. "The Lost Boys."

A. I forgot about the boys.

THERAPIST. She never got over it, they say.

BOY. She doesn't even try, they say.

NINA. How long has it been?

DETECTIVE. Long enough.

B. She's had time.

DOCTOR. She needs to get out more.

THERAPIST. She needs to try harder.

BOY. She needs to not think about him so much.

C. Didn't *she* leave *him*?

B. But he was supposed to come back.

A. He promised.

NINA. And he never came back?

B. He never came back.

BOY. And then –

DOCTOR. Did you hear –?

C. Oh, it's terrible –

THERAPIST. In the middle of everything –

A. Her father left.

NINA. Where did he go?

B. Another town.

C. Away from her.

A. Away from her mother.

THERAPIST. It was too much.

C. Some men can handle more than others.

A. Her brothers left too.

DETECTIVE. But she stayed.

BOY. She's still in that room.

A. The room where she met him.

C. I feel sorry for her.

B. Don't.

WENDY. The first time I saw him

> I was wearing a blue nightgown my mother bought me.
> The fabric was still stiff and a little bit scratchy,
> but it was so pretty I didn't care.

> I give myself eight minutes a day to think about him.
> To remember.

> Then I catalog my thoughts, when I finish thinking them –
> The things I want to forget.
> The things I want to remember.
> The things I want to have around but not have inside of me.
> I don't have a formal system.
> I put them in all kinds of things.
> Not in files, or boxes –
> Nowhere people would suspect.

> I put them between the pages of books.
> Behind paintings on the wall.
> Under loose floorboards.
> I sew them into the lining of coats.

THERAPIST. It seems to me, Wendy, that you have endowed your childhood bedroom –
> "The Nursery" –
> With an awful lot of importance.
> So much of the identity you've created for yourself is based in that room.
> It's okay to go slow.
> I know change is difficult.
> Honor your own healing process.
> But you have to start somewhere.

Go for a walk around the block.

Say hi to someone you've never seen before.

Did you know –?

On average, you have to meet forty people before you make

One lasting connection.

Why don't you try to make one lasting connection?

WENDY. I have lasting connections.

THERAPIST. A new lasting connection.

WENDY. Forty people seems like a lot.

THERAPIST. You'd be surprised at how quickly they can add up.

Especially if you leave the house.

Come on, Wendy.

Show me how good you can be at following steps.

Forty people.

Just try.

>   (**WENDY** *meets forty people.*)

A. One.

WENDY. Hello, I'm Wendy Darling.

B. Two.

WENDY. Hi, my name is Wendy.

C. Ten.

WENDY. Nice to meet you.

A. Twenty.

WENDY. It's not easy.

You could do it in one day if you really wanted to, but that's not leaving any room for a potential connection.

You can't rush these things.

B. Twenty-seven.

WENDY. It's rare to meet someone with the same level of investment.

Most people don't really like to stop and adjust their plans.

C. Thirty-four.

WENDY. But you never know.
   That's what they say.

B. Forty-two.

WENDY. Forty-two?
   It didn't work?

A. Sometimes it doesn't.

B. You can't plan things like connection.

C. Why not?

WENDY. But I tried so hard.

A. Sometimes it happens when you least expect it.

B. That's what they say.

C. I hate when they say that.

A. But sometimes –

   *(A **BOY** appears.)*

BOY. Hey.

WENDY. Hey.

B. Sometimes it's true.

   *(The **BOY** smiles at **WENDY**.)*
   (She smiles back.)

C. How do you know when it's a lasting connection?

A. It depends.

   *(**WENDY** and the **BOY** move closer.)*

C. On what?

B. How long he stays.

   *(**WENDY** and the **BOY** hold hands.)*

A. How much he knows.

B. How much *you* know.

C. How long is long enough?

B. How much is too much?

A. It depends.

C. On what?

>*(A room with a bed – not Wendy's room.)*
>
>*(**WENDY** is lying down with the **BOY**.)*

WENDY. This is nice.

>*(The **BOY** smiles at **WENDY**.)*
>
>*(He gets out of bed then leans down to kiss her.)*
>
>*(She goes in for more, but he pulls away.)*

Wait.

Come back.

BOY. Later.

WENDY. Where are you going?

BOY. Away.

WENDY. Why are you going?

BOY. Because.

WENDY. That's not a reason.

Hey.

What's wrong?

BOY. Nothing.

WENDY. You're lying. I can tell.

BOY. Wendy.

You don't have to pretend.

WENDY. What do you mean?

BOY. It's – when we kiss.

I can't feel you.

It's like you're not there.

Or like you're kissing someone else, far away.

Not me.

Kissing you is like kissing a memory.

WENDY. That's silly.

BOY. No.

It's not silly.

It's the way I feel.

And I don't want to feel that way anymore.

Can you even remember what I look like, when I'm not here?

WENDY. You're beautiful.

BOY. What color are my eyes?

(Silence.)

Let me know. If you figure it out.

WENDY. Figure what out?

(He is gone.)

Are they blue?

Or is that someone else?

C. The first time I saw him, I saw his shadow first.

B. His lips were chapped.

C. His eyes were blue.

A. I gave him a kiss before I knew what it felt like.

C. What it meant.

B. And now I know.

C. But now it feels different.

A. Now it means different things.

C. The first time I saw him, the room was dark –

B. Except for a single pool of light from the moon outside the open window.

A. It looked like he was the only person in the world.

C. He shone.

B. I noticed.

A. I met him when we were both very young.

B. When we were enchanted with the possibilities of our lives.

C. It was around the time I stopped pretending to be scared of boys –

A. And became actually scared of them.

B. We shaped one another –

C. We consumed one another –

A. The way that only very young people can.

C. I told him stories.

B. He loved stories.

WENDY. I wanted him to see –

There is a world inside me, too.

There is a world that has nothing to do with him.

But he always liked the stories about him best.

(The nursery.)

*(***WENDY*** and the ***LOST BOYS*** – ***SLIGHTLY***, ***TOODLES***, ***NIBS***, and ***CURLY*** – sit in a comfortable, cuddly pile.)*

(More of the cardboard boxes are assembled.)

My mom doesn't understand.

NIBS. Neither does mine.

WENDY. You don't have a mom.

NIBS. Exactly.

WENDY. She's turning my room into an office

And she's pretending like it's

"For My Own Good."

TOODLES. Maybe it is.

*(***WENDY*** gives ***TOODLES*** a look.)*

Maybe it isn't.

WENDY. She should be the one packing.

If that's what she wants.

CURLY. Are you still seeing that guy?

WENDY. No.

He left.

Everybody leaves.

Do you think it's me?

NIBS. Never.

TOODLES. You're perfect.

WENDY. *(Pleased.)* Oh, stop it.

CURLY. You're a delicate little flower. Some boys just can't
appreciate that.

WENDY. I don't think I'm delicate.
  Am I delicate?

CURLY. Like, mentally delicate.

TOODLES. Emotionally.

WENDY. I did it, though.
  I followed the steps.
  I tried.
  That must count for something.

NIBS. Definitely!

CURLY. You're doing so well.

SLIGHTLY. Aren't you supposed to be out doing something
today?
  Meeting more people?

WENDY. I couldn't bear the idea of everyone being together
without me.
  It's so rare these days that we're all in the same place.
  I hate it.

CURLY. Me too.

TOODLES. Me three.

NIBS. Me four.

> *(Beat.)*

> *(They all look at* **SLIGHTLY.**)

SLIGHTLY. Me five.

TOODLES. Is it part of growing up, do you think?
  Seeing your friends less?

WENDY. My mom doesn't have any friends.
  I always swore I would never be like her, ever.
  Maybe I'll run away.
  Stay with one of you and not tell her –
  Not until she's really sorry.
  Nibs, you have an extra room!

> *(***NIBS** *and* **CURLY** *exchange a look.*)

NIBS. I don't think that's a good idea.

WENDY. Oh.

NIBS. I'm sorry, Wendy.

I love you. I do.

I just

Sometimes – I need a break.

> *(Silence.)*

SLIGHTLY. You can stay with me, if you want.

I don't need a break.

WENDY. It was just a silly idea.

> *(Beat.)*

Everybody always leaves me

But I can never seem to do the leaving.

> *(Beat.)*

He said

He can't

Feel me.

He says

It's like I'm kissing someone else.

NIBS. Oh.

Well that kind of makes sense.

WENDY. How does that make sense?

CURLY. You've always been kissing someone else.

> *(An echo of a memory –* **WENDY** *and* **PETER** *in Neverland, years ago – inserts itself into the conversation somehow.)*
>
> *(Maybe we only hear their voices.)*
>
> *(Maybe there's some kind of magic that lets the past and present physically coexist for a moment.)*

WENDY. I want to give you something.

PETER. I'll take good care of it.

WENDY. How about a kiss?

PETER. You're going to want it back, aren't you?

WENDY. No.

I want you to keep it.

(The memory dissolves.)

NIBS. You and Slightly kissed.

Slightly, did you feel it?

WENDY. That was a New Year's Eve kiss.

It doesn't count.

SLIGHTLY. I counted it.

WENDY. Well, I didn't.

SLIGHTLY. Maybe that's your problem. You don't count things.

WENDY. I don't have a problem.

NIBS. You have a lot of problems.

WENDY. You do!

TOODLES. We all do.

CURLY. I, for one, am very well-adjusted.

WENDY. *(A realization.)* Peter still has my kiss.

I gave it to him.

That's it!

What if no one else can really have it, while he does?

What if that's why I've had such a hard time?

NIBS. Wendy. No.

TOODLES. Are you sure you're not just feeling extra sad because you have to leave the nursery?

CURLY. People don't usually make great decisions when they're sad.

WENDY. What if I spend the rest of my life without being felt?

I want to be felt.

I want to feel.

I have to find him.

C. I thought I saw him yesterday morning.

A. His lips were chapped.

B. His eyes were blue.

A. His eyes were brown.

C. His eyes were green.

> (**WENDY** *with the* **DOCTOR.**)
>
> *(He listens to her heart.)*

B. His hands were the first hands I ever held in that special way.

C. The way that's not like holding hands with your dad.

A. The way that gives you butterflies.

C. It was around the time I stopped caring if my shoes were comfortable.

B. All those feelings inside.

C. Just from hands.

A. Who knew?

DOCTOR. All vital signs are good.

Heartbeat a bit fast.

Nothing to be concerned about.

Everything's normal.

WENDY. I'm telling you – there's something wrong with me.

Can you check again?

DOCTOR. You do know I'm a pediatrician.

You're not a child anymore.

It's time to find another doctor.

WENDY. Some patients see pediatricians well into their mid-twenties.

A doctor is a big decision.

You can't rush these things.

> *(Beat.)*

DOCTOR. Say "ah."

WENDY. Ahhhhhh.

> *(The **DOCTOR** checks her tongue with a tongue depressor and continues the examination.)*
>
> (**WENDY** *with the* **THERAPIST.**)

(They hold playing cards.)

THERAPIST. Are you sleeping?

WENDY. Some.

THERAPIST. At night?

WENDY. No.

THERAPIST. How's your throat?

WENDY. Sore.

THERAPIST. Have you been closing the window when it's cold?

*(**WENDY** says nothing.)*

Well then.

WENDY. I didn't think it was your job to judge me.

THERAPIST. Why don't we just go back to our game.

Do you have any Twos?

WENDY. No.

(Beat.)

THERAPIST. Wendy.

What are we supposed to say?

(Silence.)

Instead of "No"

In this game.

...

We're supposed to say "Go Fish."

Do you remember?

(Beat.)

It's good practice

To follow rules.

WENDY. Do you have any Princesses?

THERAPIST. There is no such thing as Princesses in cards.

I know sometimes rules feel silly –

WENDY. What feels Silly is playing Go Fish past the age of twelve.

THERAPIST. Structure is a useful tool –

WENDY. It doesn't work!

Your Structure.

Your Tools.

I met forty people and I tried and you're wrong and I'm going to find Peter.

I decided.

I have to.

THERAPIST. I understand why you think that might help.

But it's important you don't regress.

Implementing structure takes time.

WENDY. I tried time.

That didn't work either.

THERAPIST. It might feel worse before it feels better, but it will feel better.

It might take longer than we think it should.

That's okay.

But structure does help. Time does help.

They give us containers for our feelings.

WENDY. You're lucky.

To have feelings that fit inside containers.

That sounds nice.

A. I had never felt those kinds of feelings.

B. We shaped one another.

C. We consumed one another.

B. I had never felt those kinds of feelings.

A. They were so big, it felt dangerous.

(**WENDY** *and the* **LOST BOYS**.)

(*All of them thinking really hard.*)

(*After a moment –*)

CURLY. (*An unbelievably great idea.*) Maybe we –!

(*He decides his idea is actually terrible.*)

Never mind.

(*They go back to thinking.*)

WENDY. I could put up fliers!

TOODLES. What would they say?

WENDY. "Urgent –

Wendy Darling seeks Peter Pan."

NIBS. Hmmmm.

No.

People will think that's a metaphor.

CURLY. You're kind of a type.

TOODLES. "Have you seen this boy?"

NIBS. Maybe...

WENDY. "I need you."

TOODLES. I'd stop and look at that.

CURLY. It's nice to be needed.

NIBS. Sometimes it makes me tired.

SLIGHTLY. I don't know how effective fliers will be.

CURLY. You never know who could see them.

TOODLES. I have a question.

WENDY. What?

TOODLES. I don't understand how Peter kept your kiss.

SLIGHTLY. That's not a question.

TOODLES. Sorry.

WENDY. Don't apologize when you have nothing to apologize for.

TOODLES. How did Peter keep your kiss?

There.

Now it's a question.

CURLY. Like, a kiss is a physical thing, right?

But it's also an idea?

It's like the wind.

You can see the wind, you can feel it, you can hear it, but you can't keep it.

TOODLES. Yeah!

You can't *not* feel the wind, when it blows.

WENDY. Kisses are different than weather.

NIBS. Look.

> *(**NIBS** kisses **CURLY**.)*
>
> *(Then he kisses **TOODLES**.)*

Did both of you feel me?

CURLY. Yep.

TOODLES. Uh-huh.

NIBS. See?

WENDY. You still don't understand.

You kissed them, but you didn't Give them your Kiss.

Everybody has one.

One kiss that's theirs alone.

It's usually at the corner of the mouth, but I've seen them other places, too.

> *(The **LOST BOYS** look at her blankly.)*

Have you never seen one?

You guys.

God.

You never notice anything.

NIBS. Didn't he give you a kiss, too?

WENDY. He *kissed* me, he didn't give me The Kiss.

We called a lot of things kisses in the beginning.

Acorns, thimbles.

A strawberry, once.

CURLY. Okay so to be clear –

You're trying to get your actual kiss.

Not something else *called* a kiss.

WENDY. Correct. Mostly.

TOODLES. I am very confused.

WENDY. I can't let your confusion get in the way of my quest.

SLIGHTLY. Oh, now it's a quest.

WENDY. Life is a quest.

TOODLES. That's a pretty thought.

And a scary one.

SLIGHTLY. It seems like maybe you should do some more experiments before you settle on this.

Like, kiss one of us, and we'll see if we can feel it.

WENDY. No.

Then it's a different kind of kiss altogether.

I'm not interested in scientific kissing.

NIBS. Good try, though.

SLIGHTLY. Shut up.

TOODLES. I don't think fliers would hurt.

WENDY. That's the spirit!

CURLY. He might not have it anymore.

It was a really long time ago.

SLIGHTLY. A kiss isn't something you keep.

WENDY. None of you understand.

CURLY. We knew him, too.

WENDY. ...

I know.

NIBS. Sometimes it seems like you forget.

TOODLES. I miss him.

CURLY. He was our family.

It was our home.

SLIGHTLY. We left him behind. Everyone he knew.

TOODLES. I bet he was so sad.

NIBS. Maybe he cried.

TOODLES. I liked it when he cried.

NIBS. Me too.

TOODLES. It was pretty.

SLIGHTLY. We want to help, Wendy, we always want to help you.

But I

Don't know if finding Peter is the best way to do that.

WENDY. It's the *only* way to help me.

If you really want to, you will.

TOODLES. I'm kind of scared.

WENDY. Oh, don't be scared!

It'll be fun!

An adventure.

NIBS. We don't really like those anymore.

WENDY. Of course we do!

CURLY. I like sleeping in.

WENDY. We can retrace our steps.

Look for fairies?

I don't know.

TOODLES. We could talk to the other girls!

(Beat.)

(He was not supposed to say this.)

WENDY. What other girls?

(A terrible silence.)

TOODLES. Oh.

I thought you knew.

I thought she knew!

*(**WENDY** replays years of her life through a different lens.)*

A. Do you remember –?

B. Those girls.

C. The others.

NINA. Why was Wendy the famous one?

A. Instead of them?

C. Because of those Boys.

B. Remember?

DOCTOR. Three children disappear.

DETECTIVE. Seven come back.

THERAPIST. Because of her family.

BOY. Because she never got past it.

C. But wait –

A. Did you hear about the fliers?

B. Wendy Darling.

C. *That* Wendy Darling.

NINA. She hung up fliers.

DETECTIVE. She's looking for him.

B. For Peter.

WENDY. I give myself eight minutes a day to think about him.

But thinking isn't doing,

And doing takes more time.

A. What will They say?

DOCTOR. The others.

B. When she finds them.

BOY. If she finds them.

NINA. What will he say?

THERAPIST. When she finds him.

C. If she finds him.

> (**WENDY** *and* **SLIGHTLY** *in the nursery.*)

SLIGHTLY. You're wasting your time, looking for these girls.

You're just treading water.

Because you're scared.

WENDY. I'm not scared.

SLIGHTLY. If you really want to find him, you have to go there.

WENDY. I can't fly anymore.

Not many happy thoughts.

And we're all out of pixie dust.

No fairies in sight.

SLIGHTLY. I thought of something –

> (**SLIGHTLY** *produces a jar of fireflies.*)

WENDY. Are those

Fireflies?!

SLIGHTLY. They're not fairies, but they might work.

I still don't think finding him is a good idea

But if that's what you want to do...

(He takes one out, squashing it to get its luminescence.)

WENDY. Don't kill it!

SLIGHTLY. Bugs have very short lives, and at least this way they have purpose.

WENDY. They had a purpose before.

Just because you don't know what it was doesn't mean it didn't exist.

Maybe this isn't a good idea.

I need more time to prepare.

To think of what I'm going to say.

SLIGHTLY. I think you've done plenty of preparation.

WENDY. Remembering is different than preparing.

SLIGHTLY. To fly, you have to forget.

WENDY. Anyway, it probably won't work.

Do you think it's going to work?

> *(**SLIGHTLY** interrupts **WENDY** by taking her face in his hands.)*
>
> *(He wipes some of the light onto her face, gently.)*
>
> *(He lets his hand hover for a moment longer than he should.)*

SLIGHTLY. Do you feel any floatier?

WENDY. Not really.

Not yet.

> *(Beat.)*

SLIGHTLY. Wendy.

I have something I want to tell you.

Before you fly away.

> *(**WENDY** starts to open the jar for more fireflies.)*

WENDY. Maybe we need more.

SLIGHTLY. Hey.

I think about you.

All the time.

WENDY. Because we're together like, all the time.

SLIGHTLY. That's not why.

I don't think about you the way I think about anyone else.

You are so wonderful, sometimes I feel like I could drown.

Do you know what I mean?

(*Beat.*)

(**WENDY** *grabs the jar of fireflies and studies it so that she has somewhere else to look and something to do with her hands.*)

WENDY. When I find him –

What do you think I should say?

(*Beat.*)

SLIGHTLY. Did you hear me?

WENDY. ...I

did hear you.

Thank you.

But this is hardly the time or the place to talk about anything like that.

Besides, I'm not even that wonderful.

It's just an idea you've got in your head for some reason.

SLIGHTLY. For a lot of reasons.

And it's not just an idea.

You

Shine.

I –

Have you ever

Thought about it?

Thought about me?

(*Beat.*)

WENDY. You know too much.

There's nowhere to hide.

SLIGHTLY. I think that's a good thing.

(He steps closer to her.)

WENDY. Do you think he would grow up if I asked him to?

SLIGHTLY. …

Wendy, I don't know.

WENDY. You knew him better than anyone.

You two were always together.

SLIGHTLY. Didn't you ask him already?

WENDY. People change.

SLIGHTLY. No.

I don't think he would.

I don't think he would do anything for anyone other than himself.

(Beat.)

*(***WENDY*** hands ***SLIGHTLY*** the jar of fireflies.)*

(She does not look at him.)

WENDY. Flying isn't real anymore.

This was a stupid idea.

(An office.)

*(The ***DETECTIVE*** works at his desk.)*

Hello.

(Beat.)

Do you remember me?

DETECTIVE. How could I forget the famous Wendy Darling?

WENDY. I'm not famous anymore.

DETECTIVE. Oh, I'd say you are. In some circles, at least.

WENDY. Which circles?

DETECTIVE. Detective circles.

Academic circles.

Those kinds of circles.

WENDY. Those are very different circles.

DETECTIVE. I'd say they're very similar circles.

    The nature of the two fields.

    They're circular.

    Circular circles.

    The past affects them both a great deal.

    History.

B. He already knew how to say things I would hear again, later.

C. Other boys had to practice making promises.

A. They came so easily to him.

WENDY. I need your help.

    I need to find him.

DETECTIVE. Great.

      (Beat.)

WENDY. What's the first step?

DETECTIVE. You think I can just snap my fingers and find him?

    Years and years

    I kept track.

    Took note of the signs

    Identified the patterns

    Adapted to the changes.

    Traveled the distance.

    Waited.

    Start again.

    Repeat.

    It didn't work.

    Case is closed.

WENDY. Re-open it.

    I found out about the others.

DETECTIVE. There haven't been any missings that follow his pattern in quite some time.

    The last one took place within a year after you returned.

WENDY. What was his pattern?

A. He's just a boy.

B. That's what I would say to myself,

C. If I were someone other than myself.

DETECTIVE. It doesn't matter anymore.

WENDY. Of course it matters.

Everything matters.

C. Everything sounded so new then.

DETECTIVE. You sabotaged things.

You gave your Doctor and your Therapist false information.

You slept with the window open – even though it gave you a cold –

Just In Case he came back.

Your mother put a lock on it – you broke the lock.

No one knew how.

WENDY. I was a child.

I didn't know any better.

B. He said he'd be back.

A. He said I should wait.

WENDY. Please.

Please, I –

Help me.

> *(Pause.)*

> *(The* **DETECTIVE** *softens.)*

DETECTIVE. If I were you

I'd start with the letters.

> *(Letters everywhere.)*

> *(Maybe they fall from the sky.)*

> *(Or maybe they were there all along, and* **A**, **B**, *and* **C** *pull them out from pockets, books, under floorboards, behind paintings.)*

> *(All kinds of places we don't expect.)*

DOCTOR. People mail all kinds of letters to all kinds of places.

BOY. To all kinds of people.

DETECTIVE. A name with no address.

THERAPIST. Addresses that don't exist.

DOCTOR. Santa Claus – The North Pole.

THERAPIST. Peter Pan – Neverland.

BOY. Second star to the right.

DETECTIVE. Straight on 'til morning.

A. He said once that he didn't get any letters.

B. So I thought it might be nice for him to get one now.

A. Did he get it?

C. Did he read it?

B. Did he think less of me for sending it?

C. Maybe he didn't get it.

B. I'll send another one.

A. Put more stamps on it this time.

C. Print the return address very clearly.

B. So he doesn't get lost when he comes back.

A. So he can find me.

C. So he can find me.

B. So he can find me.

>*(**WENDY** gathers an armful of letters.)*

>*(**A**, **B**, and **C** become **CALLIE**, **CORA**, and **KRISTA**.)*

>*(**WENDY** makes her way to them.)*

>*(They are all onstage at the same time, but their conversations happen in different times and places.)*

>*(**CALLIE** folds clothes or hangs them on a laundry line.)*

>*(**CORA** might read the newspaper or drink a cup of coffee.)*

>*(**KRISTA** might be at work or sitting on a park bench reading a book.)*

CORA. Why are you making such a big deal out of it?

Didn't you have fun?

Wasn't it magical?

WENDY. But what if I never get to experience magic again?

What if that's all there is?

CORA. Most people never experience magic at all.

Most people never fly.

We're the lucky ones.

Get over it.

KRISTA. So what –

Are you trying to start some kind of support group?

WENDY. Oh god no.

Nothing like that.

KRISTA. I mean

I only asked because

That could actually be really nice.

CALLIE. Oh.

You're Wendy Darling, aren't you?

*(All the girls stare at **WENDY**.)*

(Beat.)

KRISTA. Your hair's different.

Did you cut it?

CALLIE. I remember that picture they used when you were gone.

WENDY. That was a long time ago.

CALLIE. But your eyes are the same.

WENDY. Eyes are always the same.

Size, at least.

From when you're born until you die.

CALLIE. That's a myth, actually.

They grow until you're about thirteen.

They stop and everything else starts.

CORA. I just think it's really childish, that you blame him.

WENDY. I'm not childish.

I'm grown-up now.

CORA. But you don't want to be.

You're all slouchy and scared about it.

Sit up *(Or "stand up," dependent on staging.)* straight and be a woman.

CALLIE. I thought I saw him last week in the library.

I wanted to call his name, but I'm very sensitive to library rules.

WENDY. Did he ever come back for you?

CALLIE. Once.

KRISTA. Twice.

CORA. Nope.

CALLIE. You?

WENDY. …

He said he would.

KRISTA. He said a lot of things.

WENDY. Did you leave anything there?

CORA. What –

Did you *pack*?

To go on a spontaneous adventure?

KRISTA. I left a sweater, I think?

WENDY. Do you miss it?

KRISTA. It's just a sweater.

WENDY. Sweaters are important.

KRISTA. I have other sweaters.

I bought new ones I like even better.

WENDY. I left a kiss.

KRISTA. Oh.

CORA. Oh.

CALLIE. Oh.

WENDY. Well, I didn't *leave* it, I gave it to him.

CALLIE. I still leave clothes on the line for him.

Just in case.

A coat, if it's cold.

WENDY. I do the same thing.

Some shirts, some pants – there were always holes in his, and he doesn't know how to fix them.

KRISTA. I think he's probably fine.

He can buy his own pants now.

WENDY. Oh sure.

At all the Neverland department stores.

With all the pirate gold.

KRISTA. ...you don't know?

WENDY. Know what?

CORA. You didn't know.

CALLIE. I'm so sorry.

KRISTA. He's not there anymore.

He grew up.

WENDY. Oh.

> *(Time stops.)*
>
> *(Time speeds up.)*
>
> *(Time fragments into a million pieces.)*

How do you know that?

CORA. Everyone knows.

CALLIE. This girl told me.

WENDY. When?

Why?

CALLIE. Apparently it happened pretty soon after you came back.

Like a year or so.

KRISTA. I saw him.

CORA. He had some girlfriend, I think?

Pretty close to here?

WENDY. What?

Who?

CORA. Does it really matter?

WENDY. Why did you write him a letter?

If you knew he wasn't there to get it?

KRISTA. I guess it wasn't really a letter to him.

It was a letter to who he used to be, from who I used to be.

CALLIE. You're going to be fine.

I wasn't for a long time, but now I am.

(Beat.)

*(**WENDY** studies **CALLIE**.)*

WENDY. Why do you still leave clothes for him, if you're fine?

*(**NINA** rushes in, clutching a flier.)*

(The other girls disperse.)

NINA. Excuse me!

Hi!

Wendy!

Wendy Darling!

Oh my goodness I can't believe it's really you.

I have read everything about you since forever.

WENDY. This is not really a good time.

NINA. No, wait –

I saw your flier –

I have information you want.

I promise.

I just

Can I ask you some questions first?

WENDY. …two minutes.

NINA. Great.

I love a ticking clock.

I'm Nina.

Hi.

Okay.

So I'm doing this paper on you.

Not on you, like, specifically you –

People like you.

WENDY. What kind of people?

NINA. You know.

Like.

Kidnapped people.

WENDY. Oh.

Well, that's not what I am.

NINA. That's actually a really common attitude.

Like.

People always think they're the exception, they never think they're the norm.

Isn't that interesting?

WENDY. But there *is* always an exception.

Right?

NINA. Sometimes things are exactly how they seem.

I like that.

I like it when things just

Are.

Anyway.

No one's talked to you in any official capacity

besides the police, right?

No interviews. No press conference.

WENDY. Just my friends – you probably know them as the "Lost Boys."

NINA. I guess they're not lost anymore.

...sorry. Bad joke.

Anyway.

I interviewed some of them, too.

WENDY. Oh.

I didn't know that. They didn't tell me.

NINA. They're super fascinating

and I know that's like a big reason why you're so famous, bringing them back the way you did, but my paper is really supposed to focus on female victims.

WENDY. I'm not a victim.

NINA. Of course. I didn't mean to –

WENDY. Just ask the questions or whatever.

NINA. Sure. Yes.

Were you scared?

WENDY. No.

...

Yes.

(*Beat.*)

NINA. We're almost the exact same age, did you know that?

Of course you didn't know that, you just met me.

Two days apart.

I'm younger.

So when it happened –

I remember seeing your picture

And thinking,

"That girl looks like she'd be my friend."

Your face was everywhere, you and your brothers.

And my mom really hammered that point home, you know?

As a cautionary tale.

"You think you're so grown-up and can take care of yourself?

This girl is only two days older than you, and look what happened to her – Snatched right up."

(*Beat.*)

Can you tell me about the first time you saw him?

(**WENDY** *and the* **LOST BOYS**, *minus* **SLIGHTLY**.)

(*The* **LOST BOYS** *pack nursery items into the cardboard boxes.*)

(**WENDY** *writes in a notebook.*)

NIBS. You're right – I *did* want to spend my afternoon packing things that aren't mine – how did you know?

WENDY. I'll help in a minute, I'm just –

I have to keep track of the different stories I got from the different girls.

TOODLES. How is that
Going?

WENDY. Progress is being made.
No thanks to any of you.

CURLY. Are you
Okay?

WENDY. Yes.
Yes!
Just because I don't tell you guys everything doesn't mean I'm not okay!
You don't tell me everything!
You don't tell me about the other girls –
You don't tell me you've been giving interviews –
You don't tell me he grew up –
Apparently you don't tell me much of anything!
But that doesn't mean *you're* not okay!
So stop asking me if *I'm* okay just because I'm not telling you everything!

    (Pause.)

NIBS. First of all, Slightly didn't know.
So don't be mad at him.

CURLY. He's very noble.

WENDY. Not the point.

TOODLES. Hey, Wendy?
Can I ask you something?
...actually, I don't know if it's a question.

WENDY. Go ahead.

TOODLES. Remember when we were in Neverland?

WENDY. *(Duh.)* ...I do.

TOODLES. And do you remember when you asked us to come back here with you and grow up?

WENDY. Those are both questions so far.

TOODLES. Yeah!

...

I don't know what to say now.

CURLY. Just keep going, you're doing great.

TOODLES. Well like, when you asked us?

You seemed so confident?

You made growing up seem like a really great thing?

And I mean, it is.

Most of the time.

I like driving cars and buying things and eating ice cream whenever I want.

Even when it's not great, I'm still glad we came back with you.

But

You just seem really mad and sad most of the time.

You never tell us stories anymore.

You don't seem like you want to be here or grow up or anything, really.

(Beat.)

WENDY. Sorry.

TOODLES. That's okay.

WENDY. Everything was different in my head than it was actually doing it.

NIBS. Yeah, but you've had a long time to adjust.

And out of everybody, you already had the most experience growing up.

So why are we still so much better at it?

WENDY. I don't think you can be "better" at something like growing up.

There aren't any grades.

NIBS. I mean, there kind of are.

I exercise.

I eat well.

I have hobbies.

I have friends who aren't you guys.

You don't do or have any of that.

WENDY. That's a really mean thing to say.

NIBS. It's just the truth.

WENDY. The truth can be mean.

NIBS. No, I don't think so.
The truth is the truth.
The truth is facts.
Facts don't have emotions.

CURLY. We just don't like seeing you sad
All the time.

WENDY. If I stop being sad, I stop remembering him.
It hurts to remember, but it hurts more to forget.

TOODLES. But if you forget, how do you know if it hurts?
You don't.
Because you forgot.

WENDY. Memories are all we have to fill us up inside.
When we forget, we empty out.
And now that he's grown-up –
I thought it was a bad thing at first.
I thought all I wanted was my kiss back,
But I want more than that.
When I find him, we can finally be together.

(Beat.)

CURLY. Wendy, this is exhausting.

WENDY. What is?

NIBS. You.

(Beat.)

WENDY. Is this about Slightly?
Are you mad at me because I don't want to be with him instead?

CURLY. Nobody's mad.

NIBS. I'm a little mad.

CURLY. That isn't useful right now, Nibs.

NIBS. No one is better than Slightly.

CURLY. I know that.

TOODLES. We just think

    Maybe

    It would help you grow up if you weren't around us so much.

WENDY. No.

    No!

    You're wrong!

    I need you.

TOODLES. We also think

    Maybe

    It would help *us* if you weren't around us so much.

CURLY. You need to need us a little less.

WENDY. Oh.

(Beat.)

CURLY. We want to help you.

    But only if you really want to be helped.

NIBS. Unless

    You're ready to be done with everything.

    No more Peter.

(Pause.)

WENDY. I can't.

TOODLES. Oh, Wendy.

NIBS. I told you.

*(The **LOST BOYS** leave.)*

*(**WENDY** does not move.)*

B. Did you hear –?

A. They left.

B. Those boys.

C. Just like her father.

B. Just like her brothers.

C. Just like Peter.

A. But she left Peter, remember?

B. To come back here.

C. He was supposed to come back.

B. He didn't.

A. Will They come back?

C. Those Boys?

B. Everyone leaves her.

C. Why?

A. There's no real reason.

B. There are a lot of reasons.

C. Maybe it's her fault.

B. Poor thing.

A. I feel sorry for her.

C. Don't.

> *(Wendy's* **MOTHER** *sits by* **WENDY***'s bed in the nursery.)*

WENDY. It looks different in here. Did you paint the walls?

MOTHER. No, dear.

WENDY. Oh.

They look –

Painted.

MOTHER. It's wallpaper, dear.

WENDY. Maybe that's it.

MOTHER. The same wallpaper since before you were born, dear.

WENDY. You keep saying that word, and it's starting to sound like nothing.

> *(Beat.)*

MOTHER. I made your bed earlier.

WENDY. You didn't have to do that.

MOTHER. Extra tight, the way you like it.

Wrapped up like a mummy.

WENDY. I don't like that anymore.

MOTHER. Since when?

WENDY. Since it started feeling like a trap.

MOTHER. Well then, I'll loosen it.

    (Pause.)

    (**MOTHER** *begins to pack.*)

WENDY. You don't need to do that.

    (**MOTHER** *continues to pack.*)

MOTHER. I was thinking we could go away this weekend.
  Just the two of us.

WENDY. Why?

MOTHER. For my birthday.

    (Beat.)

WENDY. Oh.

MOTHER. You forgot.

    (Pause.)

  How are your friends doing?

WENDY. My friends?
  You mean the boys you practically raised?
  Those friends?

MOTHER. They're always welcome.
  I love to see them.
  But
  I do wish you would let me know when they sleep over.

WENDY. They're family.

MOTHER. Actually, they're not family.
  They're dear friends, and I care about them very much.
  But they're not family.

WENDY. They're my family.

MOTHER. I'm your family.
  But I'm sure you would have never forgotten Toodles's birthday.
  Or Nibs, or Curly, or any of them.

WENDY. Slightly.

MOTHER. What?

WENDY. You're missing Slightly.

MOTHER. The point is, Wendy, that you need some emotional boundaries.

You give things too much importance.

WENDY. Somebody's back in therapy.

"Emotional boundaries."

God.

>   *(Silence.)*

What.

MOTHER. I didn't say anything.

WENDY. But you want to.

MOTHER. I saw your fliers.

Why on earth are you looking for him?

WENDY. I need closure.

MOTHER. Sometimes we have to move on without closure.

Things aren't always tied up neatly in this life.

WENDY. Did you know there were other girls?

>   *(Beat.)*

MOTHER. I did.

WENDY. Everyone knew but me.

I feel so stupid.

MOTHER. I thought it would hurt you.

I know you – clung to the idea of being the only one.

Being special.

WENDY. I did.

>   *(Beat.)*

He has something of mine.

MOTHER. What does he have?

WENDY. My kiss.

MOTHER. Your kiss.

WENDY. Why didn't you ever give yours away?

MOTHER. What do you mean?

WENDY. Your kiss.

It's right there.

Everyone can see.

Some people might pretend they can't out of politeness, but they can.

I'm old enough now, you can tell me.

MOTHER. It wasn't that I didn't want to give it away.

I tried.

It just has a mind of its own.

WENDY. I don't believe that.

Or else it would have gone away when you were young and foolish and didn't know better.

MOTHER. Every kiss is different, I suppose.

WENDY. Not even to Dad, though?

MOTHER. I tried. I really did.

I wish –

Sometimes I wish I was more like you.

(**WENDY** *and* **NINA** *in the nursery.*)

NINA. I know I owe you some information.

I just thought it would really add an extra something to my paper

if I got a sense of the environment.

Where it happened.

And since you said you have to move out soon…

WENDY. I mean

The room will still be here.

It just won't look like this.

And I'll still be here.

Just downstairs.

For now.

NINA. It must be a really emotional time.

WENDY. I haven't really noticed.

I've been busy.

But it's nice that you're here.

The only girl I see regularly is my mother.

NINA. Why is that?

WENDY. I think I'm scared of them.
   Girls.

NINA. You're a girl.
   Are you scared of yourself?

WENDY. Do you have other questions or something?

        (Beat.)

NINA. You were there for nine days?
   In "Neverland"?

WENDY. Time works differently there –
   The seasons –
   It's always winter when he's gone.
   Even if he just flies away for a night.
   So it was longer there.
   Years.

NINA. Or so it felt.

WENDY. Or so it felt.

        (Beat.)

NINA. And you haven't seen him since?

WENDY. No.

NINA. Not even recently?

WENDY. That's the whole point.
   That's why I've been talking to you.
   You told me you could help.

NINA. The last time you saw him, did he say / anything about –?

WENDY. He said he would come back.
   He said I should wait.

NINA. You never saw him in passing, on the street?

WENDY. I've had a lot of false alarms.
   I thought I saw him once on the train.
   But he doesn't take trains.
   He flies.

NINA. Not if he grew up.

WENDY. I guess you're right.

It's hard to imagine him on a train.

He's so impatient.

Trains are so slow.

NINA. I don't know why he never came back for you.

He talked about you all the time.

WENDY. Wait.

What?

NINA. You weren't first.

You weren't last.

Either of those would be easier to understand.

WENDY. I don't –

Did you

Go there too?

NINA. No.

He asked me to, but I wasn't up for it.

I'm very delicate.

I don't like adventure.

But I liked him.

So I convinced him to stay.

WENDY. How did you do that?

NINA. I asked him.

WENDY. So did I.

NINA. I had never felt those kinds of feelings.

They were so big, it felt dangerous.

I thought we didn't have secrets.

I knew all about Neverland, and I knew all about you.

I knew about the others.

But one day he just –

Left.

I couldn't find him, I couldn't reach him, I –

When I saw your flier...

When I realized who you were...

I thought he had gone to find you.

You were there.
You know what it was like.
What he was like.

>   *(Beat.)*

WENDY. It was just a place where a bunch of kids played pretend.

NINA. It had to be more than that.

>   *(Beat.)*

WENDY. What's he like now?

NINA. He's not going to be what you think.

WENDY. What if he is?

NINA. Nothing stays the same forever.

B. Running was my favorite.

A. Living in a city, you don't get to run that way.

C. We tore through the forest like we were being chased.

A. But sometimes we *were* being chased.

B. And sometimes we got caught.

C. It was so scary.

B. I got a splinter in my foot one time.

A. It hurt so bad.

WENDY. But I pretended like it didn't.

C. My favorite was pretending.

WENDY. But you can only pretend so long.

A. There weren't any grown-ups.

B. Nobody knew how to get the splinter out.

C. It hurt to walk.

B. It hurt to run.

A. I missed home.

WENDY. I missed my room.

B. I started to forget the way my mother smelled.

C. And I was afraid of what else I was capable of forgetting.

WENDY. I liked flying the best, but not for the reasons you'd think.

I didn't like going up.

I liked coming down.

The certainty of the ground.

> (**WENDY** *and* **SLIGHTLY**.)
>
> (*The nursery is becoming more and more empty.*)
>
> (**SLIGHTLY** *packs.*)

You don't have to help me pack.

I can do it by myself.

SLIGHTLY. I know you can.

> (*More packing.*)
>
> (*More silence.*)

It looks so sad in here.

WENDY. Rooms can't be sad.

SLIGHTLY. Of course they can.

> (*Beat.*)

I can't believe it's your last night in the nursery.

I remember my *first* night in the nursery –

When we came back with you?

I thought this room was the happiest place I'd ever been.

WENDY. That's so silly.

Think about where you came here from.

All the magic.

SLIGHTLY. I do.

This is better.

> (*Beat.*)

WENDY. Have you talked to them lately?

SLIGHTLY. I have.

They're good.

They miss you.

WENDY. You could just go with them.

SLIGHTLY. I know.

WENDY. I was horrible to you.

SLIGHTLY. That's all right.

WENDY. No.

It's really not.

> *(Beat.)*

SLIGHTLY. I promised.

After your dad –

Do you remember?

I said I'd never leave you.

> *(A moment.)*
>
> *(**WENDY** nods.)*
>
> *(They keep packing.)*
>
> *(Quiet.)*
>
> *(**SLIGHTLY** picks up some clothes.)*
>
> *(Stops.)*

Whose are these?

WENDY. Mine.

SLIGHTLY. No

They're not.

WENDY. You don't know all my clothes.

SLIGHTLY. Wendy.

Are these

For him?

WENDY. ...just in case he needs them.

SLIGHTLY. He doesn't, though.

He doesn't need you to leave him clothes.

He doesn't need you.

Period.

WENDY. Look.

I know you like me

Or whatever.

But just because you're jealous doesn't mean you can try and stop me from doing what I need to do.

SLIGHTLY. I am not trying to stop you.

    I am trying to help you.

WENDY. It doesn't feel like help.

    And even if it was, which it's not, no one is asking you to help.

    I can do stuff by myself.

SLIGHTLY. I know you can.

WENDY. Good.

SLIGHTLY. But I know you're scared.

WENDY. I'm not scared.

    Why would I be scared?

SLIGHTLY. I think we're all scared!

    All the time!

    Every Time I look at you, I'm terrified!

    You make me so mad, and so sad, and so confused –

    But I wish I could drink the air you breathe.

    Those are big, scary feelings to feel

    But I Feel them.

WENDY. I just –

    I want to feel those things too, but I can't, I –

    That is what I'm trying –

    Don't you –?

    I –

    Once I find him and we –

    Once I have my kiss back and –

    He –

    Someday maybe I –

    When I can feel new things –

    I just –

    It's –

    I don't –

SLIGHTLY. *(Trying to calm her.)* Hey –

        (Pretending can be really hard.)

        (**WENDY** *grabs* **SLIGHTLY** *and kisses him.)*

(He kisses her back.)

(Oh boy, does he kiss her back.)

(They kiss for a long, long time.)

(Then they stop kissing.)

(They look at each other.)

(A moment.)

I felt that.

And I bet you did, too.

(He leaves.)

*(**WENDY** is alone.)*

(A long quiet.)

WENDY. Did you hear –?

Do you know –?

That girl –

Wendy –

What about her –?

I'm sick of her.

All these years –

All that waiting –

All this looking –

She said she couldn't Feel, but she lied.

She could

and she did

and it was scary.

It was too scary.

It was easier to Hide.

She hid behind a lot of things.

She hid behind the past –

She hid behind those Boys –

But now they're gone

Just like everyone else.

Why?

Because of her.

What did she do?
So many things.
I feel sorry for her.
Don't.

She kissed one of them, they say.
She kissed him
And she felt it.
And he –

She never sleeps, they say.
She can't stop crying, they say
She's obsessed
She's a mess
I

I give myself eight minutes a day to think about him.
To remember.
Uninterrupted. Without feeling guilty or mad at myself.
It seems a reasonable amount of time –
Eight is my favorite number.
I've whittled it down over the years.
Maybe one day it'll be five minutes.
Then two.
Then no minutes at all.

He said come away with me
He said forever
I said
That's an awfully long time
and I guess I thought we were just saying pretty words
Even though it felt big and real.
We were kids, you know.
Kids say things.
He was a boy.
I was a girl.
Boys make big promises.

Girls know better than to believe them,
but they go along with them anyway.
I went along with him anyway.

The first time I saw him –

It doesn't matter when I first saw him.
Before I saw him, I was making him up.
The last time I saw him, he said he'd be back.
He said I should wait.
And I did.
I do.
Because he said I should.
But I can't anymore.
I won't.

> (**PETER** *has entered without* **WENDY** *seeing.*)

PETER. Why not?

> (**WENDY** *startles but does her best to hide it.*)
>
> (*A long pause.*)
>
> (**PETER** *is not the kind of person who feels the need to fill silences.*)
>
> (**WENDY** *collects herself.*)
>
> (*From the moment* **PETER** *enters, the very air is different somehow.*)
>
> (*Things slow down.*)
>
> (*An atmosphere of glass.*)

I heard you were looking for me.

WENDY. How.

PETER. The stars were talking about it one night.

WENDY. No, they weren't.

PETER. Maybe you forgot how to listen to stars.
You used to know.
They liked you better than me.
They still ask about you.

I thought I saw you

A week or two ago.
And another time, a month before that.
I thought I heard my name on the street
Once or twice.
It sounded like your voice.

WENDY. So it's true.

You grew up.

PETER. So did you.

WENDY. You knew that already.

PETER. It's different seeing it.

WENDY. You said you wouldn't.

PETER. I changed my mind.

WENDY. How?

PETER. It just happened.

WENDY. Why?

PETER. I just did.

WENDY. When?

PETER. I'm not good at keeping track of time.

WENDY. Those aren't answers.

PETER. Those are my answers.

(Pause.)

WENDY. How's your shadow?

PETER. My shadow?

WENDY. That's how we met, remember?

It flew away, and you were sad, and I fixed it for you.

PETER. Oh.

I forgot about that.

WENDY. I thought that's how you'd remember me –
The girl who fixed your shadow.

PETER. I don't need help remembering you.

(Beat.)

It was just a trick.

I wanted to get closer to you.
Make you talk to me.
And I was scared to ask.

WENDY. You never seemed scared to me.

PETER. I'm good at pretending.

(*Beat.*)

WENDY. How did you get in here?
I thought the door was locked.

PETER. Locks can't keep me out.

WENDY. That's what they're for.

PETER. What happened to your imagination?

WENDY. I got rid of it.

PETER. That was a silly thing to do.

WENDY. Your eyes are different.

PETER. They changed color.

WENDY. Why?

PETER. I don't know.
I'll ask them.

WENDY. Don't make fun of me.

PETER. (*Sincere.*) Oh, Wendy.
I'm not.

(*Beat.*)

WENDY. I think you should leave.

PETER. You've been looking for me, and now I'm here.
Why would you want me to leave?

WENDY. I changed my mind.
Like you changed yours.

PETER. No, you didn't.
You're just scared.

WENDY. Don't tell me what I am.
Please go.

PETER. I don't want to.

WENDY. Well, I want you to.

And my wants are just as important as yours.

And this is my house.

PETER. It's your parents' house.

I remember the wallpaper.

Why are you still here?

Aren't you supposed to leave?

Find a new place to live?

Isn't that part of growing up?

WENDY. I *am* leaving.

And you don't get to ask me those questions.

PETER. I have one.

A place to live.

WENDY. Where is it?

PETER. Ah, somewhere.

I'm not good with the names of things.

WENDY. You can't remember where you live?

That's not cute.

That's troubling.

PETER. You're no fun.

WENDY. I'm plenty of fun when I want to be.

You don't know me anymore.

PETER. Can you please be sweet to me?

Just a little?

You make me nervous.

(*Beat.*)

WENDY. I met Nina.

PETER. That's good.

I think she's wanted to meet you for a long time.

She knows how much you meant to me.

WENDY. Why does she get to know that?

I don't even know how much I meant to you.

PETER. You do, too.

You know.

(*Beat.*)

WENDY. She said you wouldn't be what I think you are.

PETER. What do you think I am?

WENDY. Why did you choose her?

PETER. I don't know.
Lots of reasons.

It was time.
It was getting harder to fly.
I kept remembering things.
To fly, you have to forget.

It was a windy night.
I was tired by the time I got to her window.
She was wearing yellow flannel pajamas, with the tiniest flowers on them.

She asked me to stay.
It sounded nice.

WENDY. I asked you to stay.

PETER. Did you?

WENDY. I begged.

PETER. I don't remember that.
I do remember you wanting to come back here.
I remember you leaving.
I remember everyone leaving.

I remember being lonely.
And for a while that was fine.

But then...

(*Beat.*)

WENDY. You said you'd come back.
I waited.

PETER. I know.

(*Beat.*)

WENDY. How many other windows did you go to?
In the dead of night, when parents were asleep?

PETER. I went to your window.

WENDY. It doesn't matter.

    It didn't mean anything.

PETER. Maybe not to you.

WENDY. Of course it meant something to me!

    I was talking about *you*!

    I didn't even stay long.

PETER. You could have stayed as long as you wanted.

    I told you that.

    Don't you remember?

    Your nightgown was the softest blue I'd ever seen.

WENDY. You were covered in dirt.

    There are stains in the carpet that never came out.

    You never even apologized.

PETER. I'm sorry.

WENDY. It doesn't matter now.

PETER. Everything matters, Wendy.

    I learned that from you.

        (Beat.)

    I'm sorry I hurt you.

    But you've hurt me plenty, too.

        (Beat.)

WENDY. I think you have something that belongs to me.

PETER. What?

WENDY. I think you know.

PETER. ...I don't.

WENDY. You *must* know.

PETER. *You* must be mistaken.

WENDY. I need it back.

    I need my kiss.

PETER. Your kiss?

    Oh.

    No.

    You can't have that.

WENDY. Why not?

PETER. Because it's mine.

Because you gave it to me.

WENDY. I changed my mind.

PETER. You can't do that.

WENDY. You changed your mind about growing up.

PETER. I didn't give that to you.

WENDY. You've had it for a very long time.

Now it's time to give it back.

PETER. But I need it.

WENDY. Peter.

PETER. Wendy.

Darling.

Your name is still so pretty to say.

…

The truth is.

I used it.

Used it all up.

You'll have to get one somewhere else.

People are awfully careless with their kisses –

They leave them lying around everywhere.

WENDY. Those aren't mine.

PETER. But if you take some from different people, you can put them all together

And after a while, it makes something new.

It's kind of nice.

You can't get back what you give

But you keep giving.

You keep taking.

And then you make something new

So other people can take from that and make something new, too.

WENDY. But I thought there was One Kiss.

One that was more special than the rest.

PETER. I don't know.

Maybe there is.

Or maybe that's just what people say.

> *(Pause.)*

WENDY. Do you think I'm stupid for believing it all?

Just some stupid, gullible girl?

PETER. I never thought you were stupid.

Didn't then, haven't since.

WENDY. I think I was stupid.

PETER. I think you were brave and remarkable.

Maybe a touch bossy, but always tender.

And never, ever stupid.

I didn't even know what kisses *were*.

You knew so much.

So many stories.

I always felt like you'd realize how empty I was compared to everything inside you.

> *(Beat.)*

Hey.

WENDY. What.

PETER. I'm sorry I don't have your kiss anymore.

> *(Pause.)*

WENDY. You could give me a new one.

> *(Beat.)*

PETER. Is that what you want?

WENDY. I

Need to get the other one out of my head.

End on something different.

> *(Beat.)*

PETER. Okay.

WENDY. Okay?

You won't want it back?

PETER. Of course I will.

I'll think about it.

Wonder how it's doing.

But as much as I'll want it back, I'll want you to keep it even more.

Come here.

WENDY. No.

You come to me.

> *(He goes to her.)*
>
> *(They are very close.)*
>
> *(A moment.)*

PETER. What are you going to do with it?

> *(Beat.)*
>
> *(**WENDY** thinks.)*

WENDY. What you did with mine

I guess.

Give it to someone else.

I mean

I'll try.

I get scared.

PETER. Just pretend you're not.

WENDY. No.

I think I'm done with that kind of pretending.

I think it's okay to be scared.

> *(**WENDY** reaches out and traces **PETER**'s jaw lightly with her fingertip, then retracts her hand.)*
>
> *(**PETER** touches **WENDY**'s face.)*
>
> *(Her hair.)*
>
> *(They kiss.)*
>
> *(It is soft and simple.)*
>
> *(Beat.)*

Oh.

PETER. What?

WENDY. Nothing.

> *(Beat.)*

I'm – really glad I saw you.
But you should leave now.
I have some packing to do.

PETER. ...

Are you sure?

WENDY. Yes.

> *(After a moment, **PETER** leaves.)*
>
> *(He wants to look back, but he does not look back.)*
>
> *(**WENDY** is very still.)*
>
> *(She looks around the room.)*
>
> *(She packs a box.)*
>
> *(This should take as long as it takes.)*
>
> *(She looks at the open window.)*
>
> *(Breathes in the breeze.)*
>
> *(She walks to the window, and closes it.)*
>
> *(She leaves.)*

End of Play

Printed in the USA
CPSIA information can be obtained
at www.ICGtesting.com
LVHW050034221223
767161LV00007B/184